SUPERS

Spaceship Stowaways

Jillian Powell

Series consultants:
Cliff Moon and Lorraine Petersen

RISING★STARS

nasen
NASEN House, 4/5 Amber Business Village, Amber Close,
Amington, Tamworth, Staffordshire B77 4RP

Rising Stars UK Ltd.
22 Grafton Street, London W1S 4EX
www.risingstars-uk.com

The right of Jillian Powell to be identified as the author of
this work has been asserted by her in accordance with the
Copyright, Design and Patents Act 1988.

Published 2007

British Library Cataloguing in Publication Data.
A CIP record for this book is available from the British Library

ISBN: 978-1-84680-312-3

Printed by Craft Print International Limited, Singapore

Contents

Characters

Miles He's smart, and always up for adventure.

Ryan Miles's best mate – he is mad about skateboarding.

Leah Erin's identical twin sister.

Erin Leah's identical twin sister!

 **Alien** He's on a secret mission to planet Earth.

Narrator The narrator tells the story.

Scene 1

Trapped!

Narrator	Miles and Ryan are alone at the skatepark. It's getting dark.

Miles   I guess it's time to pack up.

Ryan   Just one more go.
I'm going to do this air trick
if it kills me!

Miles   It might do if it gets much darker!

Ryan   Just watch this. I know I can do it.

Miles   Go on then, hurry up!

Ryan   Okay! Here we go.

Narrator Ryan rides down the skate bowl
and flips into the air.
But Miles suddenly spots something
in the sky. It looks like a spaceship
and it's coming towards them.

Ryan Well, what do you think?

Miles What is *that*?

Ryan I told you, it's a frontline 180.

Miles Not that, you muppet.
What's that thing in the sky?

Ryan What thing?
Oh, it's probably an airship.

Miles Well whatever it is,
it's coming straight for us.
Duck!

Scene 1   Trapped!

Narrator   The boys dive for cover.
They watch the spaceship glide down.
It lands in the skate bowl.

Ryan   It looks like some kind of spaceship.

Miles   Shh! Something's happening.
The doors are opening, look!

Narrator   The doors slide open
and an alien steps out.
The boys stare in shock.

Alien   Galla to Queen Ship.
Galla to Queen Ship.

Ryan   Who's he talking to?

Miles   Looks like he's on a weird
kind of phone.

Alien   Galla has landed on planet Earth.
My mission begins.

Miles   Mission?

Alien   I will not let the Queen Ship down.
             I will bring them back.
             I will look until I find them.
             I will report at hour one hundred.

Ryan   Hour one hundred?

Miles   Never mind that.
             Who's he looking for?
             What's this mission?

Ryan   He's gone, look.
             He's left the ship.

Miles   Let's go take a look.

Ryan   Are you mad? There might be
             more of them inside.

Miles   We have to get a picture.
             Just imagine. We could get the first
             photo of a spaceship!
             We'd get loads of money for it.

Narrator The boys walk towards the spaceship.

Ryan What's that noise?

Miles It's the doors! They're opening!
Let's take a look.

Ryan Don't be stupid.
It's probably a trap!

Miles I just want to see what it's like inside.

Narrator Miles steps inside the spaceship.

Miles Wow! This is major!
You have to see this, Ryan.

Narrator Ryan follows Miles.

Ryan This is a bad idea. A really bad idea.

Miles Relax. There's no one here, look!

**Leah and
Erin** There is, actually!

Narrator Miles and Ryan swing round
to see Leah and Erin.
They are identical twins.

Miles Who are you?

Leah I'm Leah.

Erin I'm Erin.

Ryan You're not aliens, are you?

Leah Do we look like aliens?

Miles Shut up, Ryan. They're obviously
not aliens. But you are twins, right?
I mean … it's amazing.
How do people tell you apart?

Erin They don't!
We play all sorts of games on them.

Leah So who are you?

Miles   I'm Miles. This is Ryan.
We just saw this thing land.
What are you doing here?

Erin   That's what we want to know.
This alien just snatched us.

Leah   He said we would do for his … mission.

Erin   We don't know what that means.

Ryan   Right. Well, I vote we get out of here
before he comes back.

Erin   Wicked idea, Ryan.
How exactly do we do that?

Ryan   The same way we came in.

Leah   You don't know about
the smart doors then.

Miles   Smart doors?

Leah   They open when they want to. And they
close when they want to, as well.

Narrator Miles and Ryan turn round
to see the doors closing.

Ryan Oh no! I told you it was a trap.
What do we do now?

Miles I'll try my mobile.

Leah You won't get a signal.

Miles She's right.
There's no signal at all.

Ryan Wait a minute!
It's that noise again.
Look, the doors are opening.

Miles Let's get out of here.
Come on, everyone!

Narrator Suddenly, they all freeze.
It's the alien.
He's come back.

Scene 2

A mission uncovered

Leah   Quick, hide!

Narrator Miles and Ryan duck down
             behind a screen.

Alien   Galla to Queen Ship.
             Galla to Queen Ship.

Ryan   (*whispering*) Queen Ship?

Miles   He's on that phone thing again.

Ryan   Shh! Listen.

Alien   I am returning to the Queen Ship.
              Repeat, I am returning
              to the Queen Ship.
              I have the females.
              I will deliver them.

Leah   That's us.

Erin   Oh, great!
              Now they're taking us
              to their Queen Ship.

Alien   I have been unable to find more.
              Repeat, I have been unable
              to find more.

Miles   More what?

Ryan   Search me.

Alien   (*to the twins*) You, get inside
              the flight shells.
              Prepare for flight.

Narrator   The twins climb inside the flight shells.
The alien goes into the control room.
There are lights flashing
on the control panel.

Miles   We have to do something.

Ryan   Like what?

Miles   Well, look. There's only one alien
and there are four of us!

Leah   There's only one alien in this pod.

Miles   Pod?

Erin   This is a pod ship.
It'll dock with the Queen Ship.
That's hundreds of pods
joined together.

Leah   With hundreds of aliens
inside them!

Miles   You mean like some
              sort of honeycomb?

Leah   Exactly. And the aliens
              are like worker bees.
              They work for the Queen Ship.

Erin   Once we dock, there will be four of us,
              and hundreds of them!

Ryan   So we have to stop this pod
              reaching the Queen Ship.

Miles   I think it might be a bit late for that.

Ryan   Why?

Miles   Just look at my phone.
              The GPS is going mad!

Narrator Miles and Ryan stare at the phone.
The pod is already shooting
through space.

Leah You two should get inside
one of these shells.
There could be a ...

Narrator Suddenly, there is a huge bang.
Miles and Ryan are thrown across
the floor.

Ryan What on earth was that?

Erin Sounds like we just docked
with the Queen Ship!

Narrator The alien comes out
of the control room.
Miles and Ryan duck down
and hide so he can't see them.

Alien Galla to Queen Ship.
Docking is complete.
Request pod entry.

(*to the twins*) We have docked
with the Queen Ship.
You will now follow me.

Ryan (*whispers*) Where's he taking them?

Miles I don't know. But we'd better
follow them.

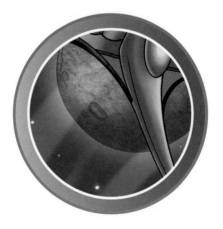

Narrator   The door to the pod opens.
It leads into another, bigger pod.
There are aliens everywhere.
The alien leads the girls away.
Miles and Ryan follow,
staying out of sight.

Miles   Is this weird or what?

Ryan   Remind me who had the great idea
of going inside that pod.

Miles   Ssh! Look where they're going.

Ryan   Looks like some kind of science lab.

Miles   I don't like the look of it.
What are all those machines for?

Alien   You will come in here.
You will remain here.

Leah   What are you going to do with us?

Erin   What are all those wires and stuff?

Alien	The tests will take place here.
Leah	What sort of tests?
Alien	Human DNA tests.
Erin	Human DNA? What for? Why us?
Alien	You are our key.
Leah	Key to what?
Alien	The key to planet Earth. You are the copy of her. She is the copy of you. Your human DNA holds the key. We will learn from you how to copy humans. Then we will replace them one by one! Our clones will control planet Earth!
Miles	(*whispers*) Did you hear that? Talk about identity theft!

Ryan   So it was twins they were after.
              Identical twins.
              That was their mission.

Miles   We have to stop them.

Narrator The alien makes the twins sit down.
              He straps them in and wires them up
              to machines.

Alien   You will not move.
              The tests will begin soon.

Narrator Lights on a control panel
              begin to flash. The alien checks
              them over, and then leaves.

Miles   Look, he's going.
              We have to get them
              out of there!

Narrator The boys head into the lab,
but the alien hears something.
He turns back.

Alien Alert! Alert!
Stowaways in Queen Ship!
Request help!

Miles Oh no! He's seen us.
Quick, run!

Narrator The boys make a dash for it.
But aliens are hot on their heels.

Scene 3
The bluff

Ryan   Where are we going?

Miles   I don't know. Anywhere,
just keep moving.

Ryan   They're catching us up.

Miles   There's another door, look.
Get into the next pod.

Ryan   Oh, no!

Miles   What?

Ryan   I think it's one of those
smart doors – look!

Narrator The door to the pod closes.
The boys are trapped.

Ryan Oh no! We've had it now.

Alien Stay where you are!
You can't get away.
Who are you?

Ryan Um … my name is Ryan.

Miles And I'm Miles.

Alien Which planet are you from?

Ryan Planet Earth.

Alien Earth? How did you get into
the Queen Ship? Answer!

Ryan Well you see, we were in the skatepark.
I love skateboarding, you see, and …

Miles And we heard you needed twins.

Alien Twins? What do you know
about the mission?

Miles   Well, nothing really.
Just that you need twins
for your … mission.

Alien   And?

Miles   And we're twins.

Narrator   Ryan has a coughing fit.

Alien   You are not twins.
Twins look alike. You do not.
You do not have the same
human hair colour.

Miles   Well, no. That's true, but …

Alien   You do not have the same
human eye colour.

Ryan   We're not a bit alike,
Miles. Face it!

Miles   Well no. That's because we are not
identical twins. There are twins,
and then there are identical twins.

Alien   So you are twins …
but not identical twins?

Miles   That's it.

Alien   I don't believe you.
What is your mother's name?

Miles and Dawn.
Ryan   Brenda.

Miles   Dawn Brendan. That's our mum.
Mrs Dawn Brendan.

Alien   If you are lying …

Ryan   No, no. We're not lying, are we Miles?

Miles   No, why would we lie?
We want to help you with your …
mission.

Alien   How can you help?

Miles   Well, you can do tests and stuff.
See how our sort of twins are different
from identical twins.
Study our DNA and that.

Alien   Twins that look so different
are of no use to us. But still,
you are here. We can use you
for tests.

Miles   That's it. That's what we thought.
There's a lot we can tell you
about twins.

Ryan   There is?

Miles   Yes. I mean he loves skateboarding.
I prefer the Xbox. I mean
identical twins sometimes dress
the same. We don't.

Ryan   No way. He wears baseball caps.
I can't stand them!

Alien   Stop babbling!

Miles   Sorry!

Ryan   Sorry!

Alien   Come with me.
We will see what the tests show.

Narrator   The alien takes Miles and Ryan
to the science lab. The girls
are still wired up to machines.

Leah   There you are! We were wondering
what had happened to you.

Miles   Sorry, we were just explaining to this …
to the … We were just saying
how we're twins too.

Erin   You two are twins?

Ryan   Yes. You know, we told you.
            How we are … twins,
            but not identical twins, obviously.

Leah   No, because you're not much alike,
            are you?

Miles   No, but never mind.
            We can still help with the tests!

Alien   Shut up, all of you!
            There is much to learn.
            You are taller than he is, yes?

Miles   Just a bit. I grew a bit faster.
            We were the same size as babies though,
            weren't we?

Ryan   I guess so. My mum …
            I mean our mum never told me.

Alien   Sit down. We will begin the first
            DNA test at once. There is no time
            to lose for the mission. Planet Earth
            has always been our goal.
            Now we have the key.
            The planet will be ours.

Narrator   The alien straps the boys into chairs
and wires them up to the machines.

Alien   I will be back shortly for the first results.
Do not try to escape.

Miles   He's gone. Thank goodness for that!

Ryan   Well, that was a great idea!
What do we do now?

Miles   Sshh! I'm trying to think.

Leah   You do realise they'll find you out?

Erin   They're testing our DNA.
They'll soon find out you're not twins.

Leah   We have to get out of here – and fast!

Scene 4

A race in space

Alien   Here are the results of the first
DNA test. They will show
if the Earth boys are lying.

Narrator The alien reads the test data.

Alien   I knew it! They are lying.
They are not twins.
They are Earth spies!
They will not escape.

Narrator The alien races back to the lab.
But just in time, Miles has found
a hatch in the wall.

Miles Hurry. It's a bit small,
but we can squeeze through.

Narrator They all find themselves
in the next pod.

Ryan Wait a minute. What's that?

Miles What?

Ryan It's your mobile. You must have
dropped it when we docked
with the Queen Ship.

Leah So this is the pod we came in!

Erin Yes, those are the flight shells, look.

Miles Where was the control room?

Ryan The alien went in here, remember?

Leah Look at all those flashing lights.

Erin I wonder what these do.

Ryan What does it say on that switch?

Miles One says D. The other says R.

Leah Try D.

Miles I tried D. It's just telling me "docking complete".

Erin Try R then.

Narrator Miles presses the switch marked R.

Erin What's that noise?
Something's happening!

Leah What does it say now?

Miles It says … "docking release".
Hold on to something!
I think it's working!

Leah Go Miles! We're getting away
from the Queen Ship.

Erin We're leaving those creepy
aliens behind!

Narrator The pod is hurtling through space.

Miles We got away! We got away
from the aliens!

Erin Cool! We'll show them!

Leah Wow! Look at that. I can see
planets and things.

Miles   Talking of things, what's that thing
I can see over there?

Ryan   It's another pod!
They've sent another pod after us.

Narrator   They all look out. They can see
another pod heading towards them.

Miles   How do you steer this thing?

Ryan   That's a good point. I mean,
we're travelling through space, right?
But how do we know
where we're going?

Leah   He's right. We might be travelling
away from Earth!

Erin   Lost in space!

Ryan   We might never get back!
We could go into one of those
wormholes, or black holes
or whatever they call them.

Miles   You're not helping, Ryan!
Look, that pod is getting closer.
We have to do something.
If it docks on to us, we'll be going
straight back to the Queen Ship!

Erin   That's worse than lost in space!

Ryan   That's even worse than a black hole!

Leah   I can see it! I can see that alien
inside the pod. They're really
close now!

Miles   Wait a minute.
What does that switch say?

Ryan   "LR redial".

Miles   Last route redial.
This is the pod we were in, right?

Ryan   Deffo. You left your mobile in here.

Leah   Hurry! They're right behind us.
They're going to dock any minute.

Miles   Last route redial … If the last route
was to planet Earth … this should
get us home. Hold on tight!

Narrator Miles presses Redial. For a split second,
the pod seems to stop. Then they
hurtle back through space.

Miles   We're on our way!
We have to be!

Leah   Isn't that the moon?
It looks like the moon … *our* moon!

Erin   I can still see them.
They're chasing us!

Miles   Well, if I'm right, there's only one
landing place!

Ryan   You mean the skate bowl?

Miles   It has to be. Last route redial,
             remember? That's where this thing
             landed the first time.

Erin   I think they're gaining on us.

Leah   What happens if they get there first?

Miles   That's not going to happen.
             We can't let that happen.

Narrator Miles presses a switch marked B.
             He just has time to make it
             to a flight shell.

Leah   My head feels funny.

Erin   I feel sick.

Ryan   What did you press?

Miles   I think it might be a booster switch.
             And I think …

Narrator There is a loud bang.

Miles   We may just have landed!

Leah   Look outside! I can see –
             I think it's a skatepark.

Ryan   We made it!
             We beat those aliens.

Miles   Let's get out of here!

Erin   What about the smart doors?

Miles   I think my booster landing
             took care of them. Look!

Narrator The pod has landed with such force
that the doors have blown off.

Ryan Don't give up the day job, Miles.
Your landing was rubbish!

Miles We left those aliens standing
though, didn't we?

Ryan What's that over there?
I don't believe it!

Leah What is it? It's not an alien is it?

Ryan No, it's my skateboard!
Hello my beauty!

Miles We just raced aliens through space
and you go on about your skateboard!
There's no way you could be my twin!

Ryan   And there's no way *you* could be *mine*!

Leah   Well, you certainly argue like twins!

Miles   Come on, we've got a story to sell
             to the newspapers!

Drama ideas

After Scene 1

- In your group, think together about what might happen next. Why has the alien captured the twins? What might he do if he discovers Miles and Ryan?
- Act out your ideas.

After Scene 2

- In your group, each choose a character from the play. Imagine the character's thoughts at the end of the scene, as the aliens chase the boys.
- Take on the role of your character, and tell the rest of the group what you are thinking.

After Scene 3

- Hotseating: Choose one person to be the alien, and to imagine events from his point of view.

- Everyone else can ask the alien questions, e.g. is he pleased with his mission so far? What does he think of the boys?

After Scene 4

- With a partner, choose a character from the play.

- One of you can be a newspaper interviewer, asking the character interesting questions about their adventure in space.
  The other person can be the character, and try to make the story sound as exciting as possible.

RISING ★ STARS